D0306375

This **Picture Mammoth** *belongs to*
Sch

Northamptonshire
DISCARDED
Libraries

D
Row, row, row your boat Gent - ly down the
3
stream. Mer - ri - ly, mer - ri - ly,
3 3 A7 D
mer - ri - ly, mer - ri - ly, Life is but a dream.

Hoist, hoist, hoist the sail
We're setting out to sea.
We're sailing to an island,
Georgie, you and me.

Leap, leap, leap ashore,
Jump onto the land.
Splashing in the water,
And kicking up the sand.

Thump, bump, humpety-bump,
Who's that on the track?
A great big friendly elephant!
Let's climb up on his back.

Flap, flap, fluttering wings,
Birds fly all around.
Hold on to the elephant's ears,
We're far above the ground.

Slip, slip, slip and slide,
Down the elephant's nose,
To see the snakes and spiders
That live down by his toes.

Up, jump, hurry along,
Clambering through the plants.
I can see the monkeys!
Let's join them in their dance.

Swing from arms, swing from tails,
Swooping through the trees.
Shaking all the flowers down
And making Georgie sneeze.
Achoo!

Push, poke, tug, and pull.
The monkeys like to tease.
They pull the tail of something big
That's hiding in the trees.

Grr, grr! What's that noise?
Oooh, it's a lion's roar!
Quick, he's chasing after us,
Let's race back to the shore.

Run, run! Find the boat
And push it out to sea.
Before the lion catches us
And has us for his tea.

For Hairy Mary
P.G.
To Hayley, with love
S.L.

First published in Great Britain in 1997
by Heinemann Young Books
Published 1998 by Mammoth
an imprint of Reed International Books Ltd.
Michelin House, 81 Fulham Road, SW3 6RB

10 9 8 7 6 5 4 3 2

ISBN 0 7497 3159 1

A CIP catalogue record for this title is available
from the British Library

Printed in Hong Kong by Wing King Tong Co. Ltd.

Row Your Boat

rhyme by

PIPPA GOODHART

illustrations by

STEPHEN LAMBERT

Row, row, row your boat
Gently down the stream.
Merrily, merrily, merrily, merrily,
Life is but a dream.

Hoist, hoist, hoist the sail
We're setting out to sea.
We're sailing to an island,
Georgie, you and me.

Leap, leap, leap ashore,
Jump onto the land.
Splashing in the water,
And kicking up the sand.

Thump, bump, humpety-bump,
Who's that on the track?
A great big friendly elephant!
Let's climb up on his back.

Flap, flap, fluttering wings,
Birds fly all around.
Hold on to the elephant's ears,
We're far above the ground.

Slip, slip, slip and slide,
Down the elephant's nose,
To see the snakes and spiders
That live down by his toes.

Up, jump, hurry along,
Clambering through the plants.
I can see the monkeys!
Let's join them in their dance.

Swing from arms, swing from tails,
Swooping through the trees,
Shaking all the flowers down
And making Georgie sneeze.
Achoo!

Push, poke, tug and pull.
The monkeys like to tease.
They pull the tail of something big
That's hiding in the trees.

Grr, grr! What's that noise?
Oooh! It's a lion's roar!
Quick! He's chasing after us,
Let's race back to the shore.

Run, run! Find the boat
And push it out to sea.
Before the lion catches us
And eats us for his tea!

Row, row, row your boat
Gently up the stream.
Merrily, merrily, merrily, merrily,
Was it just a dream?